A Walk Through Color

Jada Taylor

Inspired Forever Books
Dallas, Texas

A Walk Through Color
Copyright © 2021 Jada Taylor

Inspired Forever Books™
"Words with Lasting Impact"
Dallas, Texas
(888) 403-2727
https://inspiredforeverbooks.com

Library of Congress Control Number: 2021905726

Paperback ISBN 13: 978-1-948903-56-1

Printed in the United States of America

Disclaimer: This is an original work of fiction. Any resemblance to actual persons, living or dead, or actual events is purely coincidental.

To the reader,

Continue to find beauty within yourself,

for there is no one more beautiful than you.

Table of Contents

Introduction

Don't get caught up in the title of this book. My goal is very simple. I just want to talk. Think of this book as a walk along the riverside. It'll just be me and you. Hold my hand, and view me as a person you can always trust. Imagine the day is warm and the sun has just risen over the riverbank. As you and I set out on a journey around the river, listen to my words, and imagine them rolling off the tongue of your best friend, or favorite person. While reading, do your best to keep an open mind. Unfair perceptions and negativity have no place here. Know that at any time, you can let go of my hand and leave me, but I hope you will stay.

Let's start from the beginning. Can we agree with a simple fact that we are all human? Can we agree that life may bring challenges but each of us must find a way to persevere? In today's world, it seems we are becoming more distant than ever. The reality is that we are not bonding, interacting, or growing as much as we should be. Because of this increasing distance, it may be difficult for you to empathize with my words and experiences. Therefore, I will not ask you to understand. Beauty lies within our own humanity. We've all faced some level of personal pain in this life. What heartache have you experienced? Come, let's begin our walk. . .

A Cry Not to Be Heard

Is love equal?

Or is it measurable at all?

How do you determine how much *love* loves?

Can you ever produce the same amount of love for everyone?

Is love prejudiced? Does love stereotype, or does it judge?

What factors matter when choosing whom to love?

Is love even a choice?

What makes you love one more than the other?

And do you love because you have an abundance of love in your heart?

Or do you love them because of who they are?

And since no two people are the same, can you ever love the same way twice?

Or will you ever be loved as you once were?

After being in love, and enduring its intimacy, can you possibly feel it again?

Will love be the same when love has a different face?

Will love smell heavenly and kiss you in the morning as it did before?

Or maybe it never did, and you wish love had.

Love felt like a dream then; how do you know you're not dreaming now?

And why would love leave if love truly loved you?

Why would love make you smile and hold your hand as you cried, then leave you?

Why would . . . how could love choose any-one but you?

And how do you find love, when it no longer looks familiar?

I'm sure you've overlooked it or walked past it. Or maybe you've had a conversation with it.

But do you compare it to the love you once had . . . the love you want . . .

or the love that you've always wished for?

And because you've grown since your past love,

what love do you expect to receive?

If love is determined by character, who are you?

What love should be given to you?

Are you even deserving of love?

I mean, they do say that if it's true love, it never leaves, but how many times has love left?

They say that love does not hurt,

but aren't you hurt?

I heard that love is patient and forgiving.

So why is love still mad at you?

What did you do?

Why has love given up on you?

Only you know why . . .

And I doubt love will give you butterflies

or make your heart skip a beat as it did before . . .

In fact if you expect anything you once had,

you will spend a lifetime broken . . .

I won't say forgetting is easy, but

the past is not yours!

If it were, you'd be able to control it.

The love you once had or the love you once gave,

you are no longer, and neither is he.

We've made it to the bridge on the river. Stand with me, here in the middle of the bridge. Look at the water sway softly; absorb its beauty. Breathe in. Breathe out. Close your eyes; clear your mind. Breathe in. Breathe out. Be still; don't think. Breathe in. Breathe out. Allow your shoulders to roll back; relax. Imagine your body submerging in the river. Allow the waters to cleanse and strip you of all things. Breathe in. Breathe out. Allow the sun to warm your soul. Breathe in the life of all things heavenly, and exhale things of toxicity. Breathe in. Breathe out. Know that the past is simply a teaching mechanism. What has the past taught you? Forget what you regret, and walk in the path of what you want. The future is yours; the past is not.

We've made it along one side of the river and over the bridge. We are halfway. Will you continue this journey with me? Many will turn back now. But for those of you who find that I am human and deserve a chance, continue walking with me. You'll soon find that there's always another side.

Over the Hills

Over the hills, it's lighter, brighter, and the sun always shines there. There are clear skies, clean streets, and shiny cars there. The people are one of a kind there. They are all tall, noses in the air, with nice houses and fat bank accounts.

Over the hills, it's lighter, brighter, and the sun always shines there. There's no crime, mischief, or thieves there. There are no abandoned buildings, welfare offices, or shelters there. The grass is green, and the trees are tall there. The children are all saints, and everyone's lawn is mowed. The landscapes in their front yards are phenomenal. There are pools in their backyards, and every yard has a fence there.

Over the hills, it's lighter, brighter, and the sun always shines there. There is new development every day. More restaurants than you can imagine. Spas, shopping malls, and game rooms are all there! Then there's United, Walmart, H-E-B, and Food King there. Oh yeah, I almost forgot. There are dessert places like Smoothie King, Crumbl Cookie, Insomnia Cookies, Pie Bar, and Braum's there. There are over fifty clinics, and they even have an animal clinic there. There are car lots, party rooms, companies, and firms out there. And there's over twenty schools there.

Over the hills, they have enough money to feed every hungry child nearby.

Yet on my side of the hills, the hills cast shadows here. The hills block the sun and cause drought and discomfort here. The grass isn't green here. The streets aren't clean here. Yards are polluted, and fences are rare here. Gunshots are loud here. Buildings are abandoned, which provides a place for drug addicts to lay their heads and a place for little girls to get raped here.

There are bingo halls, game rooms, and liquor stores on almost every corner here. Which keeps the poor *poor* here. There are like six restaurants, two clinics, and four schools here. Community leaders pick up trash and mow grass here. Mothers and fathers, parents lost, misguided souls here. Teachers provide shelter and love for children here. Elderly aid wounds because no one can afford health insurance here. Single mothers team up to be supporters, doctors, counselors, and coaches to children here. Because if we don't look out for one another, no one will look out for us here.

On my side of the hill, those people who claim to be for us we never see here. And even though they claim to be from here, they no longer live here. They moved over the hills and disregard what it's like to live here. Over the hills, they say that we all have the same opportunity, but tell that to the kids who grow up fast here. Tell that to the kids who help pay bills here, single mothers who work two jobs to provide for their children, little girls who sell their bodies to provide food for their younger siblings here.

Tell that to the kids who are faced with their reality every day here.

And when you look outside and see the life that you've created for your children, remember that we didn't get that choice here. We were taught to survive here. We were taught to love and look out for one another here. We were taught to dream, although our parents can't afford college here. We were taught a bottle of pain and trauma because there's way too much to be done here. There's no time to waste.

We were taught to value ourselves, although those over the hills look down on us here. They say we will never amount to anything here. They say that we are nothing more than criminals, culprits, and thieves here. They say that the conditions on our side of town are sufficient enough here.

They protest over the hills about injustices in the world without even acknowledging the injustice here. Over the hills, they say that it's just a part of life. Everyone will have obstacles to overcome. But until they have lived here, survived the circumstances here, they will never be able to understand here! And for my twenty-three years of living, nothing much has changed here! I know the hills are to blame because they allow you to ignore what really goes on here. They allow you to blindly stereotype us while you raise your children as if this world treats us fair here. I know you donate to the hungry kids in Africa, but when will you make a change here? And I know there are hills all over the world, but open your eyes; there are no hills here . . .

As discrepancies from your past unravel, allow yourself to see things in a different light. As we all know, no one asked to be raised in the ghetto. Or stripped of opportunities because of where they live. Be mindful that growing up in the ghetto means a lack of resources, growing up fast. It is fight or flight; it is survival mode at all times. Growing up in the ghetto means watching your fifteen-year-old friends get shot and killed. Yes, it happens here. It means playing hide-and-seek because the lights are off again.

I understand that you cannot foster all of us, and I know it is not your responsibility to do so. But know that we all contribute to systemic racism. Whether it is where we choose to live or where we spend our money. If you keep shopping over the hills, you contribute to their cash flow and take from ours. If you work there, eat there, and shop there, you must know that the value will keep depreciating here.

You can no longer ignore what you know. You know that there's a difference. The sooner that you admit it, the closer we are to solving a nationwide problem. You, as a human, have a natural obligation to love your neighbor. But I guess that's why you moved there, so your neighbor looks more like you and nothing like me. You live within a community that is invitation only, and my kind weren't invited. Tell me, how do I explain to my son that we are all created equal, when he is born with two strikes against him?

I don't have to tell you that the things that you ignore only get worse over time. This you know. Be an active helper, neighbor, and leader. Do the right thing! What is the right thing, you ask?

- Tell yourself the truth.

- Identify your limitations between races.

- Challenge yourself to see humans, not thugs, criminals, or migrant workers.

- Appreciate minority contributions.

- Tell your kids the truth.

- Take time to become culturally educated.

You will find that these things will lead to a better future for all of us. If you were able to understand why I run from the cops even when I am not guilty, maybe you wouldn't shoot me. If you understood that communication is different among all races, as it is within different age groups, maybe you would realize that my tone is not aggressive and my hand gestures are not a threat.

Don't punish me because you are culturally un-aware or uneducated. As a teacher, I'll be the first to attest to the saying "You can lead a horse to water, but you cannot make it drink." Everything you need is right in front of you. Every day, I am sure you encounter more than one race. Open up; learn something new about culturally diverse individuals. All of them are worth learning about. And I don't just mean their food, so that you can manipulate it into your own. But actually walk with them as you are walking with me. Have those dif-ficult conversations. Break the barriers between races. Don't act as if they do not exist. Since we can no longer ignore these issues, let's continue this conversation.

Steel Toed Boots

Day after day, dawn to dusk, the boots are stationed by the door. Having left at 5:00 a.m. and returning after dark, they steadily varnish in the corner. The boots are weathered and worn, discolored, and damaged beyond repair.

There was a time when they glittered like gold. They were well crafted; the thread was perfectly stitched. The combination of brown, black, and caramel intertwined generously. The boots were resistant, durable, and crafted to conquer anything! But by now, they've had their fair share of obstacles. They had once been matching, but neither one is the same at this point. They are conflicted, torn between the two. They lost their shine. The souls of each are hanging on for dear life. If the wind whistles one day, the souls themselves will blow away.

Having only the support of the wall, the boots weep in the corner. Light from the window drifts in to complement the boots' imperfections. The sunken tongue of the boots reminisces on the good old days just as they are snatched and worn for another workday. They trample through rubble, dirt, and nails. And still, they carry on. They work to support both themselves and the owner, even while bleeding and crying out for help.

Despite their condition, he continues to wear them day in and day out. Having no empathy or remorse for the fact that she is tired. She is broken. He will disregard that she has been his support even when he had no one else. He couldn't care less that he is nothing without her. Even while tears are pouring down her face and her fragile heart is continuously breaking, he will not stop to comfort her. He will carry on. There was a time they shared the same room, the same bed, and the same space. Now he leaves her at the front door, stationed there, without the least bit of affection. Intimacy comes only when he needs something. She will be naive and think that maybe he does care, maybe he does love her. That will be the spark that she needs to endure one more day. But when the weather's bad and rain begins to fill the wells of her eyes, she will think back to better days, days when she was beautiful and full of life. How did she come this far? Or did that even matter? Why was she still here? She knows that he is aware of the damage that he has caused, and it will not keep him from pushing the knife even farther into her heart. Just when she feels defeat arise, he will simply throw her away and buy a brand new pair of boots. Boots that are newer, brighter, and more durable than she could ever be. Leaving her in such a condition that only a desperate man will be willing to take her. A man who has limited options. One who just needs a pair of boots to get him by . . . well, that is . . . until he can do better. He, too, along with her help, will repeat the same cycle as before. Having known her past trauma will not change his purpose for her. Nor will it distract him from his overall goal of self-improvement. He will take advantage of every opportunity. And he will do so without any empathy or regard for the fact that she is not a pair of boots.

What will happen to you next? Will you leave before you are destroyed? Will you confront the pain that caused you to be where you are? What reward are you receiving that is more important than your value and self-worth? Trust me; we've all been here before, whether it's at our job or in a relationship. Someone has taken us for granted. Of course not without our permission, but involuntarily we have all been someone's boot. We allow others to use and manipulate us because we believe that the situation at hand is better than being without. Even if this is true, I'd rather you go through it while acknowledging that you must work your way out of it. In the midst of adversity, we often degrade ourselves as others do. We forget to believe in the gifts of our character and the grace of our personality. Know this—you are who you say you are! You might believe that how people treat you is a reflection of how they feel about you. This is simply not true. People treat you according to your standards and requirements. They do what you allow them to do. Don't allow anyone to dictate, rule, or use you. You are far too great for that. Despite your circumstances, you are gifted and loved. Those who do not see you as gifted are not worthy of your presence. Know that time only heals all if you are willing to do the work to heal. The past is worth reevaluating. As you read along, identify your faults, confront your realities, and plan to heal from the things that you've experienced.

Masking Tape

He piles masking tape on the holes in my heart,

a simple apology to cover the pain he caused.

He and I both know that the tape isn't enough.

But we stay still.

Blood slowly seeps out of my heart and oozes all over my white dress.

Soon we will have matching crimson outfits.

With each blood drop comes a sturdy piece of masking tape,

each piece no stronger than the last.

He cannot repair this heart.

He will simply find another.

If this heart is worth keeping,

I cannot go to my abuser to fix

what he has broken . . .

I must take it to the manufacturer

or to the creator.

And only then will

my troubles be resolved.

In what ways do you contribute to your current situation? Who put you there? How can you get out? In one way or another, we have all experienced pain, trauma, and betrayal. Ultimately, we are the only ones who can repair ourselves. No one else can mend or fix our brokenness. It is up to us to revive the person we want within ourselves. Healing is actively consoling past trauma and pain while developing a plan of problem-solving. Some days are better than others, but working is better than bottling. Are you healed? What does healed look like? What does it feel like? Before we can answer those questions, we must identify what hurts. Why does it hurt? Most pain comes from love or the lack thereof. Tell me—what has love done to you?

The Birds and the Bees

I walked into my son's room. "Son, sit down. Let me talk to you."

I had no idea where to start. I was completely lost. My father never gave me this talk. But I knew it was time, and there was no time for turning back now . . .

"Son, look at your father . . . you are becoming a young man now. You've matured, and soon, they will sniff you out like a hunting dog. First, let me ask—have you had it?"

"Had what, Dad?"

"You know . . . it."

"Dad, I have no idea what you are talking about."

I rubbed my hand across my forehead and thought, *Man, this ain't gonn' be easy.*

"Alright, son, you are tall, dark, and handsome, just like your daddy . . . and with great looks comes great responsibility. See, they want what you got."

"Dad, who are *they*, and what do they want?"

Without saying a word, I looked my son dead in the eyes and raised my eyebrow.

"Ohhhh, okay, I got it. Yeahhh, they want what I got. And I sholl got it."

"That's right you got it, boy, cause you a Johnson! Now listen, this is how it starts—when they see you, they gonn' come up to you. You ain't even gotta approach them. I told ya, boy, you a Johnson! Act cool; don't be nervous. Just go with the flow. Now this speeds up real fast. Ain't nothing you can do about it, boy! They will be all over you, like bees on honey, but don't move. Let them do all of the work. They will rub all over your body nice and slow. Then the action begins!"

My son stood up and began stroking his hip back and forth with excitement.

"Then they will slide their hands across yours, and if they freaky like us Johnsons like 'em, they will handcuff you! Remember, stay calm; allow them to violate all of your rights. By now the lights should be dimmed. Shhh! Don't say a word. They'll climb on top of you and strip you! First the shirt, then the pants, and you know what's next, don't ya, boy?"

"Yes sir, sholl do!"

"Yeah, boy, fireworks start popping, the headboard starts knocking, and the neighbors start screaming. And right before you reach the climax, your blood pumps, your body shivers, and then *boom*! They ejaculate on your bruised and broken body. They spit on you and leave you for dead as they put their "johnson" in their pants and their badge back on their shirt. They will wipe your blood and secretions off of their shoes before going to protect and serve their people. And right before your man tries to stand to attention for another round, they will kiss you goodnight behind the bars of a life sentence."

My son returned next to me on the bed.

"All of that because I'm a Johnson?"

"No, son, all of that because you are a young black man in America."

"Aren't there some good ones, though?"

"Yeah, definitely. They are not all the same. But when those good ones are amongst those bad ones, they will not choose you over their partners. What they have is intimate. Secret. You, you're nothing but a quickie. You nothing but a one-night stand. Left to deal with the pain they caused."

"So is there any way around it?"

"Nope, it's a part of life, but remember when it happens to you, remain calm, say nothing, and let them do their job. They will rub you down, strip you, and violate all of your rights. But remember that soon it will be over, and they'll find another innocent black man to violate."

Wait! Before you let go of my hand, I do know that all cops are not the same. But that is beginning to sound like a broken record. I'm not a bad person, but I, too, have done some bad things. Before you walk away and leave me, answer this—why is it so difficult to just admit that it happens?

Repeat after me: "I am human, and because I am human, I make mistakes. My mistakes define me only if I continue to make the same ones." Think of it this way: when you see a stray dog covered in mud, hair around the eyes matted, and ribs showing, you assume that the dog is abandoned or has been mistreated. You come to this assumption without knowing the dog's circumstances or seeing the owner. So why is it that you see officers beating, killing, and forcefully arresting black people, and you still deny the fact that the cop is the abuser?

Forgive me for my lack of sensitivity. I do understand that these men are fathers, husbands, and sons. Men who put their lives on the line every day to protect our country. And trust me; I don't intend to demolish your precious memories of them. They are who they are to you. But know and understand that *that* is not who they are to us. The way you act differently around your friend is similar to the encounters we have with them, only it lands us behind bars or in a grave. I cannot tell you how many times I've had bad encounters with officers, but I can tell you how to survive getting pulled over. Keep your hands visible at all times. Don't move. Don't talk, unless answering a question. Say *yes sir, no sir*. Lower your voice. Do not make eye contact. Pray and keep praying . . . I bet these things never crossed your mind when you were pulled over. Well, it's a reality. We get this talk around age eight. Our parents can only pray that we make it to age sixteen to give us the other talk. You know, the talk you give your kids about sex. I'm not sure how it goes—I never got it.

If I can't convince you that police brutality exists, then admit that your lack of awareness may be part of the problem. While we stand here along this riverside, admit that you and others like you contribute to the acceptance of the real criminals who steal dreams from children and foster them into prison systems when you don't take accountability for your selfishness and your egotistical belief system. With accountability in mind, let's continue to explore life together. Don't worry; I will try my best to tread the waters. For I know some of you have backed out and refused to walk any further. To those who I've lost, I hope that in the future you take my hand again. I will still be here, walking by the river. For everyone who is still with me, let's continue walking and talking and learning together.

Sing Flower Sing

How could a beautiful flower

sing such a sad song?

How could a flower with such gratitude

complain about the rain?

A flower of dignity and pride

shouldn't sing this sad song.

A song of betrayal and traumatic occurrences.

For every flower withers in the winter

and grows in the rain.

Having only seen this flower in the fall,

you'd believe that pity was the most appropriate response,

but do not cry for me!

I am the coffee-brown flower

that every flower wants to be!

A flower that fought my way through all things against me.

I am a flower that made the mistake of singing the same sad song.

But there's more to me,

more to you, than the storms we go through!

See, winter comes and goes

like the rest of the seasons.

And you'd be a fool to only sing heartache.

Don't you know you've got all the good stuff?

You've been blessed, handcrafted, and kissed by a king!

You have greatness within you,

so snap out of it, and sing, baby, sing!

Don't tell me what you've been through.

Tell me who you are.

Has your flower blossomed?

Have you released petals of demons

that don't fit all you've envisioned?

Is your flower radiant,

from all the gold you've soaked in?

When will your flower sing a different song?

Fertilize your soul and

begin life where you are.

For all things work!

Even for flowers!!

Although life can be hard, beauty lies within the simple things. Life itself is a gift, given to you. If you take nothing at all from your experience with me, take these two things.

First, commonalities lie within every race. Because we are human beings, the presence of emotions lies within all of us. We have all felt broken, hurt, depressed, or oppressed in some form or another. Skin color is no reason to avoid rationalizing, understanding, or empathizing with others. As we walked the river, we talked about trials and heartache of all races, religions, genders, and demographics. I hope you found yourself in each passage, actively participating as both the victim and a survivor. As you read, I hope you were devastated yet inspired to make a change.

Secondly, because we share the essence of humanity, life is livable. The good times in life often include our times together, among friends and family. We are at our bests when we are able to share laughter, love, and trials with others. Together we rise, we fall, we jump hurdles, and we overcome obstacles. We cry, kick, and scream, and still we come out on top, together!

As we approach the end of our walk and head our separate ways, let go of my hand but never my heart. Find comfort in having a friend in me. One who understands that life is and will always be challenging. Continue to walk the river, and soon we will meet again.

Thank you for taking the time to walk with me.

This is not the end.

It is just the beginning.

About the Author

Jada Taylor, high school teacher, entrepreneur, and local artist, uses her experience as a survivor of circumstance to convey the uncomfortable differences among races. Having fought through poverty, homelessness, single motherhood, and oppression, Jada embraces her ability to understand and empathize with others. In *A Walk Through Color*, she writes metaphorical short stories to enhance relativity and commonality within demographics in hopes to educate and bridge the gap. She communicates the emotions of systematically inflicted Americans. She says, "I want my novel to start conversations, ones that are past due, conversations that we as human beings all relate to and can empathize with each other on. These conversations will lead to solving problems such as racism, discrimination, sexism, stereotypism, and classism."

Jada Taylor resides in Northwest Texas with her family as she continues to explore the truths of the river.

You can contact Jada @ jada.xxx25@gmail.com

Facebook: Jada Taylor

Instagram: Jadataylor448

Made in the USA
Columbia, SC
01 September 2021